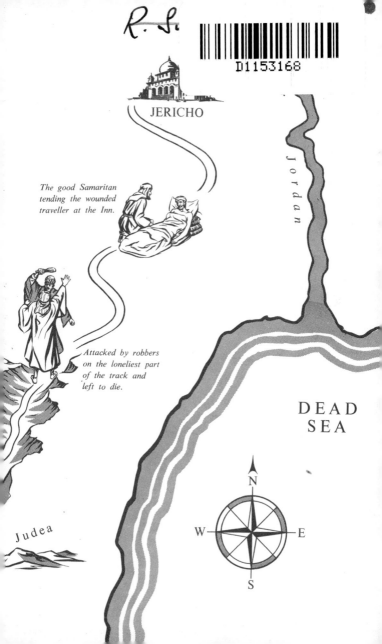

R. S.

D1153168

JERICHO

The good Samaritan
tending the wounded
traveller at the Inn.

Attacked by robbers
on the loneliest part
of the track and
left to die.

Jordan

DEAD
SEA

Judea

N
W E
S

Series 522

The simplicity, truth and beauty of these two fascinating parables: 'The Good Samaritan' and 'The Prodigal Son' have been reverently portrayed by Lucy Diamond in this little book for children.

The simple charm of these wonderful stories has been enhanced by the beautiful illustrations in full colour by Kenneth Inns.

TWO STORIES JESUS TOLD

told by LUCY DIAMOND

illustrated by
KENNETH INNS

Publishers: Wills & Hepworth Ltd., Loughborough
First published 1956   ©   *Printed in England*

THE GOOD SAMARITAN

For three years Jesus lived by the lake of Galilee, going in and out among the people, teaching them, and with loving tenderness healing their sick.

Now His ministry was nearly ended. The Feast of the Passover was at hand, and for the last time Jesus set out with His disciples for Jerusalem.

It was a long journey. They walked from Galilee into the country beyond Jordan, along the road which led through Jericho to the Holy City. They passed through towns and villages, and as they went, Jesus taught the people and healed many. Hundreds of pilgrims followed Him. At times the crowd was so great that they trod one upon another.

And always the Scribes and Pharisees were listening and waiting to catch Jesus in His speech.

7214 0154 6

Sometimes they themselves or one of their friends would ask questions of the great Teacher. These questions were always carefully thought out, so that the answer Jesus would be forced to give might seem to be something against the Law of Moses, or even words against the Roman rulers of the Jews. If they could trap Him into giving such an answer, they would at once accuse the Master, and have Him arrested.

So it happened that one day, when Jesus had stayed on His journey to talk to the people, a man on the edge of the crowd stood up and asked a question:

" Master, what shall I do to inherit eternal life? "

Now Jesus saw by his dress that this man was a lawyer—a man learned in the Law of Moses—and well able to explain it to his fellow Jews.

So very quietly He answered with another question:

"What is written in the Law? What do you read there?"

The lawyer did not hesitate. He replied at once with the words from the Law of Moses which he knew by heart:

"Thou shalt love the Lord thy God with all thy heart, and with all thy soul, and with all thy strength, and with all thy mind, and thy neighbour as thyself."

"That is right," Jesus told him. "You have answered your question for yourself. Do all this and you shall live."

The lawyer was rather taken aback. He had hoped by his question to provoke the Master to say something not strictly in keeping with the Law—some words that the Scribes and Pharisees could twist and lie about. Now he had to excuse himself for asking a question to which it was clear that he knew the answer.

He was in a difficulty.

So the lawyer pretended that it was not so easy fully to understand this Law of Moses by which the Jews ordered their lives. He knew perfectly well that to every Jew, only a fellow Jew was looked upon as a neighbour.

Yet he asked another question:

" But who *is* my neighbour? "

The question rang out, echoing across the crowd, and in breathless silence everyone listened for the answer. What would Jesus say to this persistent lawyer?

The man waited—but no answer came. It almost seemed that Jesus had forgotten him, and that His thoughts had passed on to something else. He looked around at the people sitting huddled closely together, crowding nearly to His feet, that they might more easily hear His words.

They were waiting so eagerly for Him to speak; and I think His eyes were kind and smiling as He looked upon them.

They were so like children listening for the words of the great Teacher.

He began to tell them a story.

A certain man went down from Jerusalem to Jericho . . .

A rustle of movement swept through the crowd at these words! People looked at each other, for they all knew that road from Jerusalem to Jericho. It was a very dangerous road, which passed over the Mount of Olives and by the village of Bethany, then plunged down into wild and desolate country. There it became a rough and narrow track, twisting and turning below dark, overhanging cliffs, piled up rocks, and by fearsome ravines.

Often robbers lurked behind the huge boulders, ready to spring out upon lonely travellers.

There was no house upon that road—only one poor inn where wayfarers might stay for the night if darkness overtook them.

Yes! The people in the crowd knew that road, and they knew its dangers. They could picture the solitary traveller on the loneliest part of the track as Jesus went on with the story . . .

And as the man was going he fell among thieves. A whole band of robbers rushed upon him from behind the rocks. They dragged him from his ass and stripped him of his clothing, taking all his money and the goods he was carrying. Then they beat him unmercifully, until bleeding and badly wounded he fell helpless in the dust of the road.

There they left him, and made off with their spoil towards the dark caves among the hills which made such safe hiding places for lawless men.

And the wounded man lay still—almost dying by the roadside.

Then by chance a priest passed that way, coming from his work in the Temple —his sacred work of keeping the fire alight on the altar of burnt offering, feeding the golden candlesticks with oil, and teaching the Law of Moses.

If the wounded man heard and saw him coming, he would feel that help was near. By his dress this traveller was a fellow Jew and a man of God.

But no! The priest did not even pause. He saw the poor man lying helpless in the road, and guessed what had happened. He might fare the same, and risk his life, if he stayed to help this stranger.

So hurriedly he passed by on the other side.

Again there was the sound of someone coming. This time it was a Levite—one of the men set apart to help the priests in the services of the Temple.

The Levites prepared all the corn and oil and wine used in the Temple, and they had to guard the sacred treasures.

Surely this man, set apart for holy things, would help.

The Levite drew near, and seeing the wounded man, came and looked down upon him. He saw his terrible injuries, and his misery. He saw the great rocks behind which the robbers might still be lurking, and with no other thought than to get his own self out of danger as quickly as possible, he too hastened on his way.

There was silence and loneliness on the road again. Then once more came a traveller. If the wounded man could see this wayfarer, he must indeed have given up hope. By his dress he was a Samaritan—a people whom the Jews hated—and one whom he himself at any other time would have scornfully passed by.

He would not help!

But the Samaritan was full of pity. He got down from his ass, and hurrying to the wounded man, did all he could to ease his sufferings. He gave him water. He cleansed his wounds, and pouring upon them oil and wine from his own store, bound them up.

Then gently he lifted the helpless man, put him upon his own beast, and walked beside him till they came to the inn.

All that night the good Samaritan tended the wounded traveller. He hoped that next day he might be able to help him on his way. But when morning came, it was clear that the poor man would not be able to travel that day.

The lodging at the inn was free, but food for man and beast had to be paid for.

Knowing that the robbers had taken every penny from the man they had so brutally hurt, the Samaritan went to the innkeeper and gave him two pieces of money—money worth two whole days' wages.

" This man is too ill to travel," he said, " take care of him till he is well. If you spend more than this, when I come again I will repay you."

Then the Samaritan went on his way.

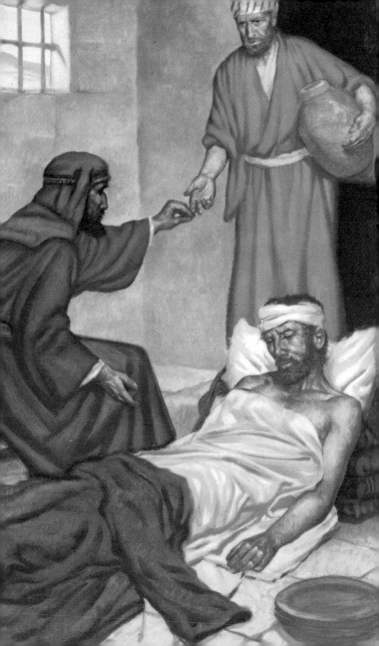

No one moved or spoke as the story ended. A new idea of love and helpfulness had crept into the hearts of those who listened.

Then Jesus turned to the man who had questioned Him, and asked:

" Which of these three do you think was neighbour to him that fell among thieves? "

The lawyer was furious that again he was forced to answer his own question for himself. He would not mention the hated name of Samaritan, or say the unlawful thing he had hoped to hear Jesus say—that one of these despised people could be a real neighbour to a Jew.

He could only mutter sulkily:

" I suppose he that showed mercy on him."

And Jesus said:

" You go and do likewise."

THE PRODIGAL SON

Jesus was still in the country beyond Jordan, journeying on towards Jerusalem, and often pausing to talk to the multitudes who followed Him. Always He preached about God's love and tenderness.

One day a group of Scribes and Pharisees stood angrily grumbling on the edge of the crowd.

" Look at these wretched publicans and sinners gathered here," they said scornfully. "This Man lets sinners come near Him, and even eats with them. What sort of a prophet can He be ? "

Jesus knew quite well what they were saying, but He went on speaking. As the Scribes and Pharisees listened, cruelly anxious to hear some word against the Law for which the great Teacher could be punished, they found He was telling a story.

There was once a man who had two sons. He was a rich man with a beautiful house and many hired servants.

This man was a very loving father, and cared tenderly for his sons. Theirs was a happy home, and it seemed that the two boys had everything they could wish for.

But one day the younger son came to his father and said:

" Father, will you give me now the share of your goods which will one day be mine ? "

The father said no word to show how hurt he felt that his son could ask such a thing. At once he divided his estate as Jewish law directed, and gave his younger son the portion which should have been his only when his father died.

The moment the younger son received his share of the money, he gathered together all his belongings, and made ready for a long journey. He hardly troubled to say farewell to those who loved him, but with never a backward glance, set off to find a new life in a strange country far from his home and friends.

He reached a city where he was quite a stranger. He knew no one there, but people soon noticed this handsome Jewish lad. He was well-dressed and seemed to have plenty of money.

Before long, many of the most careless and idle young folk of the city flocked around him, and he joyously welcomed them as friends. Soon he became their leader in a round of exciting pleasures.

The weeks and months slipped by, but the younger son had no thought of time, or of those he had left at home. He was young and rich, and the gay companions who were so eager to be his friends were all ready to feast and revel with him, and have a good time for which he paid. They joined in the wildest games, raced gilded chariots one against the other, and ended the days with banquets of rich foods and wines, all at the expense of the heedless Jewish youth who had welcomed the careless friendship they offered.

By this time, this group of wild young people were known all over the city and countryside, and all good and thoughtful folk were shocked at their wicked doings.

But by and by all the younger son's money was spent. Worse still, a terrible famine came upon the land, and food was scarce and dear.

He did not worry. He felt sure that the new friends he had made would help him now.

But no! Not one of those upon whom he had spent his money would do anything for him. Now that he could no longer feast them, and pay for their pleasures, they had no further use for him. They left him as carelessly as they had enjoyed themselves at his expense.

Then the younger son realized that he was penniless and friendless—alone in a strange country.

At last, ragged and starving, he was forced to seek for work. He tried everywhere in and around the city, but no one seemed anxious to employ him. Perhaps many of those he asked felt that they could not trust this youth who was known to have lived such a wild life.

In the end he begged and pleaded for any kind of work. He found it at last, but it was work that only the very lowest of his own people would have done.

To every Jew, pigs were unclean animals, never to be touched.

Yet when a man hired him to look after his herd of swine, the starving lad was thankful and glad to do it.

It was while he was watching the swine feed that he began to think. He had snatched up and was hungrily crunching some of the hard carob beans which the pigs were eating, when the real sense of his wicked foolishness came to him.

Here he was—the son of a good father—homeless and starving, while the very servants in his father's house had enough and to spare.

The thought of his home brought such longing that, broken-hearted, the lad wept for shame and misery.

"I will arise," he said at last, "and go to my father, and I will say unto him, 'Father, I have sinned against heaven and before you, and am no more worthy to be called your son. Make me as one of your hired servants.'"

The younger son wasted no time. He had at last realized how selfishly and cruelly he had treated his father. He left the swine to look after themselves, and turning his back upon the shame and misery of that far-off country, he started on the long and toilsome journey back to his home.

And while he was yet a great way off that loving father saw him. He had never ceased to watch and wait for his younger son to come home. Now in the far distance he knew him—knew him in spite of his dusty rags and limping feet.

How grieved he was, how full of pity, when he saw the wretchedness of the son who had for so long forgotten him.

He ran eagerly to meet him and, putting his strong, loving arms around him, he kissed the boy who had at last come back to him.

" But father," the son faltered, " I have sinned against heaven and against you, and am no more worthy to be called your son."

He could not finish all he meant to say, for his father was joyfully helping him towards the house, and calling to his servants:

" Bring out the best robe and put it on him, and put a ring on his hand and shoes on his feet. And fetch the fatted calf and kill it, and let us eat and be merry. For this my son was dead and is alive again. He was lost and is found."

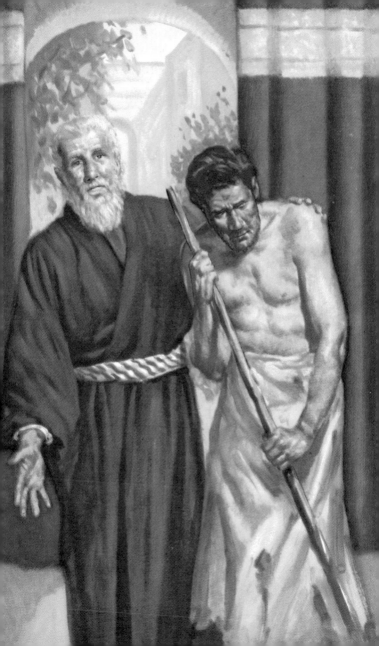

The servants hurried to do his bidding. They brought out the garments which were kept for an honoured guest, and soon the boy who was so desolate was bathed and dressed as befitted a son of the house. The fatted calf was killed, and a feast made ready to which they all sat down with happy faces and joyful hearts.

Thus the Saviour, as he told the story of a loving father who forgave his wandering son, comforted and gave new hope to any poor sinners who were listening to Him.

But the Scribes and Pharisees still stood looking on with hard, scornful faces. There was no understanding love in their hearts. I think the voice of Jesus must have been very sad as He finished the story.

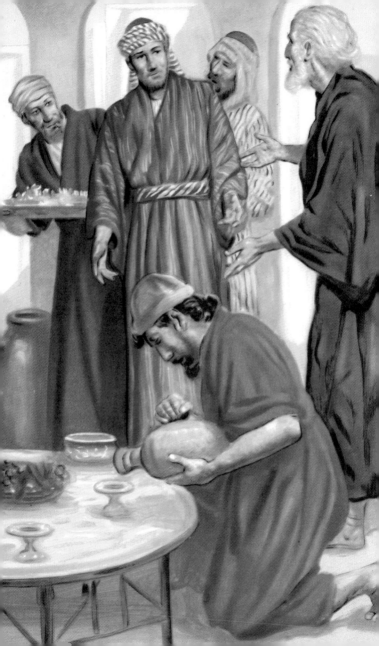

Now the elder son was busy in the fields, and knew nothing of what had happened.

When he had finished his work he turned homewards, and as he drew near the house he heard music and the sound of great rejoicing.

" What does all this mean? " he asked one of the servants.

" Your brother has come home," he was told. "Your father has had the fatted calf killed to make a feast of welcome for him."

The elder brother was furiously angry. He would not go into the house. He had no wish to meet his brother, or to join in the happy merry-making.

The father was distressed when he heard this. He went out and begged of his son to come in to the feast.

But the elder son answered bitterly, " I have served you for many years, and never have I done wrong, or forgotten my duty. But you have never even had a kid killed for me that I might make merry with my friends. "

" But as soon as this your son has come home, who left you, and wasted his time and your money on evil living, you take him back again. He is feasted and forgiven."

" My son," his father said, tenderly rebuking him, " you are always with me, and all that I have is yours. But it is right that we should make merry and be glad, for your brother was dead and is alive again. He was lost, and is found."

And he drew him towards the house.

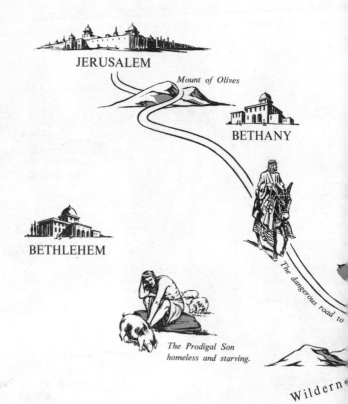

JUDEA
IN THE TIME OF JESUS

JERUSALEM

Mount of Olives

BETHANY

BETHLEHEM

The dangerous road to

*The Prodigal Son
homeless and starving.*

Wildern